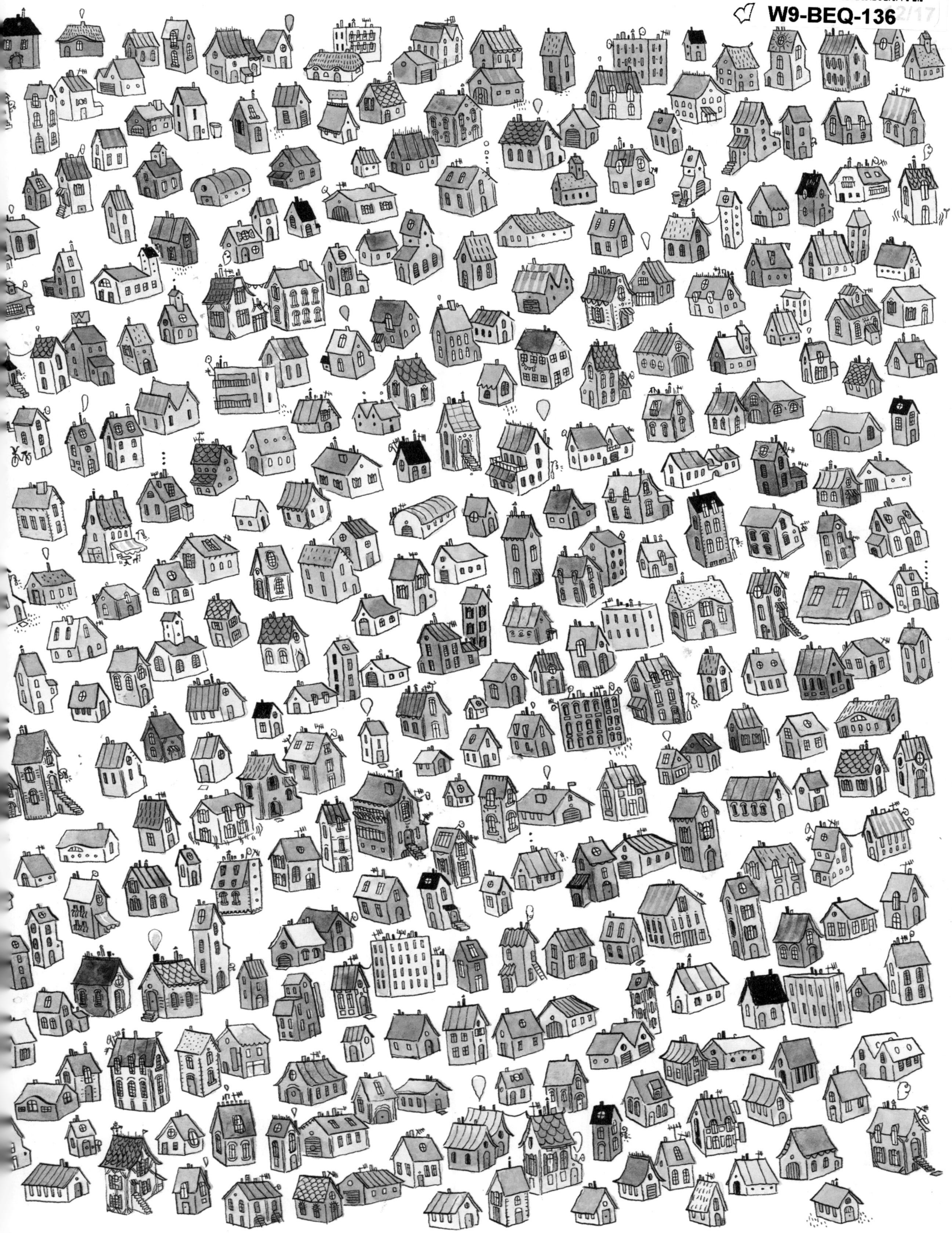

For Félix, our big everything among the little nothings.
Anne & Loïc

Text copyright © 2014 Loïc Clément, Anne Montel
Illustrations copyright © 2014 Loïc Clément, Anne Montel
Translated by Vanessa Miéville

First published in the English language in 2017 by
words & pictures, Part of The Quarto Group
6 Orchard, Lake Forest, CA 92630

A CIP record for the book is available from the Library of Congress.

ISBN: 978-1-91027-742-3

1 3 5 7 9 8 6 4 2

Printed in China

A Thousand Billion Things

(and some sheep)

Loïc Clément • Anne Montel

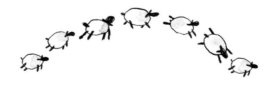

I don't like going to sleep!

Of course, you are wondering, why not?
Well, let me tell you, it's a matter of choice!

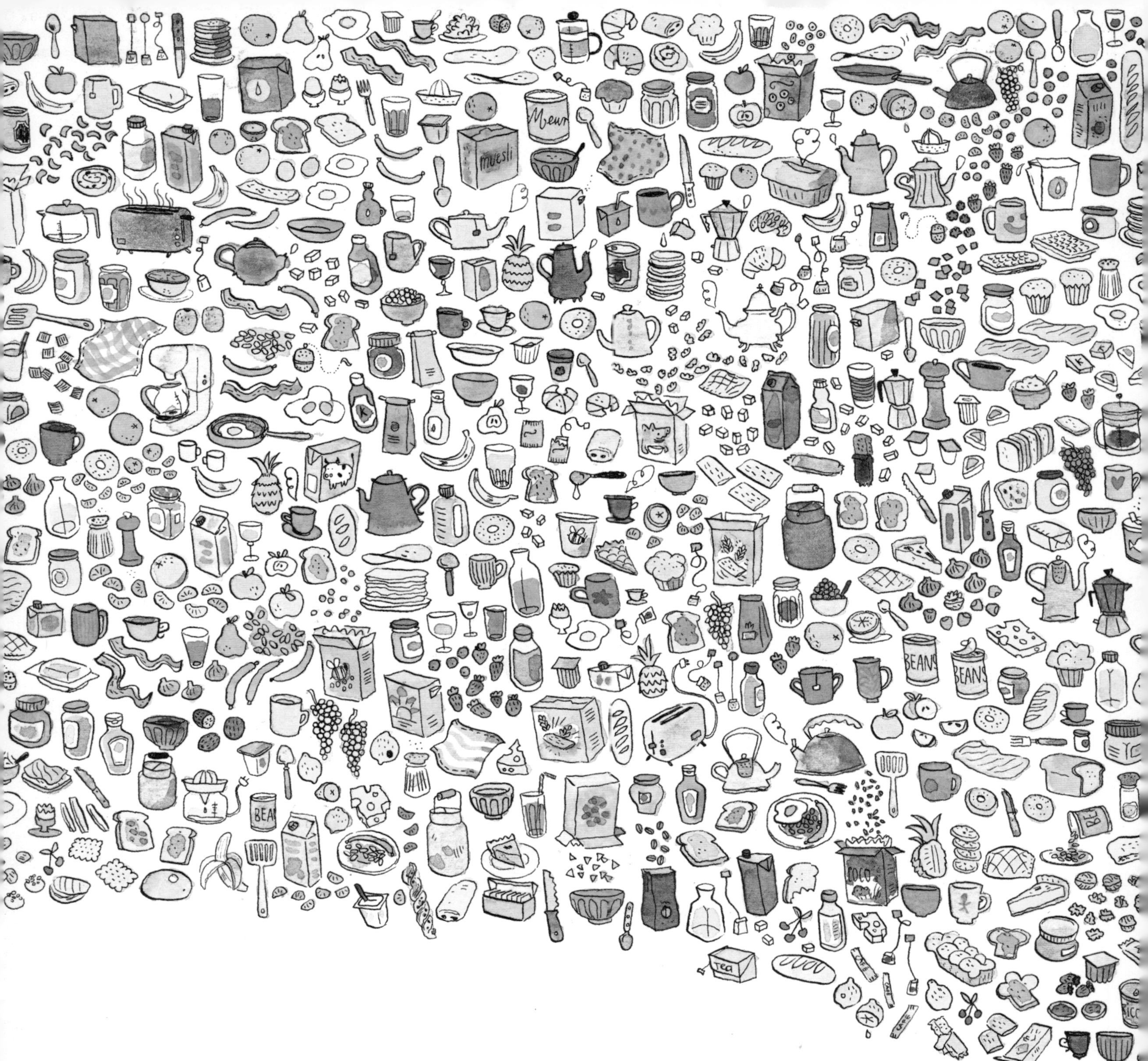

muesli
BEANS
BEANS
TEA

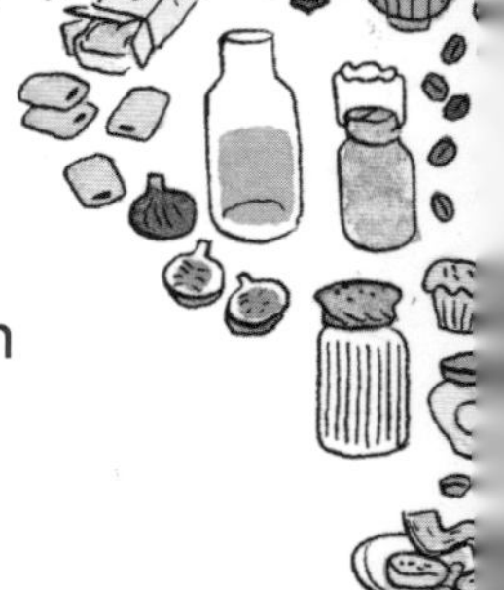

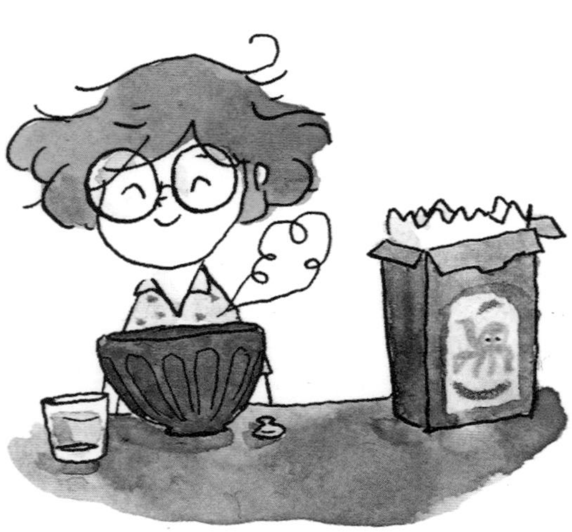

At breakfast, I get to choose between trying to butter a mountain of toast without breaking it, or drowning an avalanche of breakfast cereal in milk.

Can you find my box of breakfast cereal?

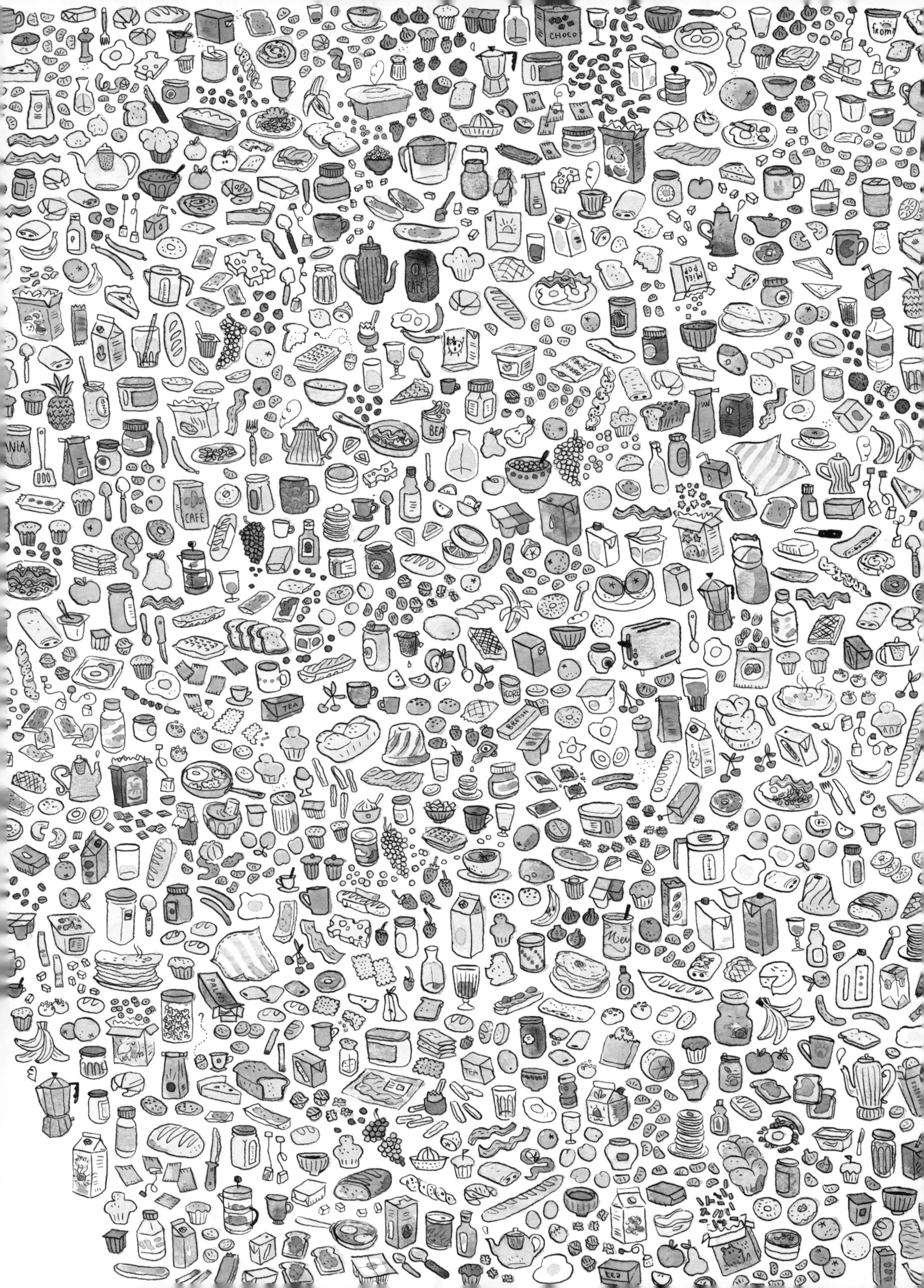
CHOCO
from?
CAFÉ
CAFÉ
TEA
BRETON
TEA

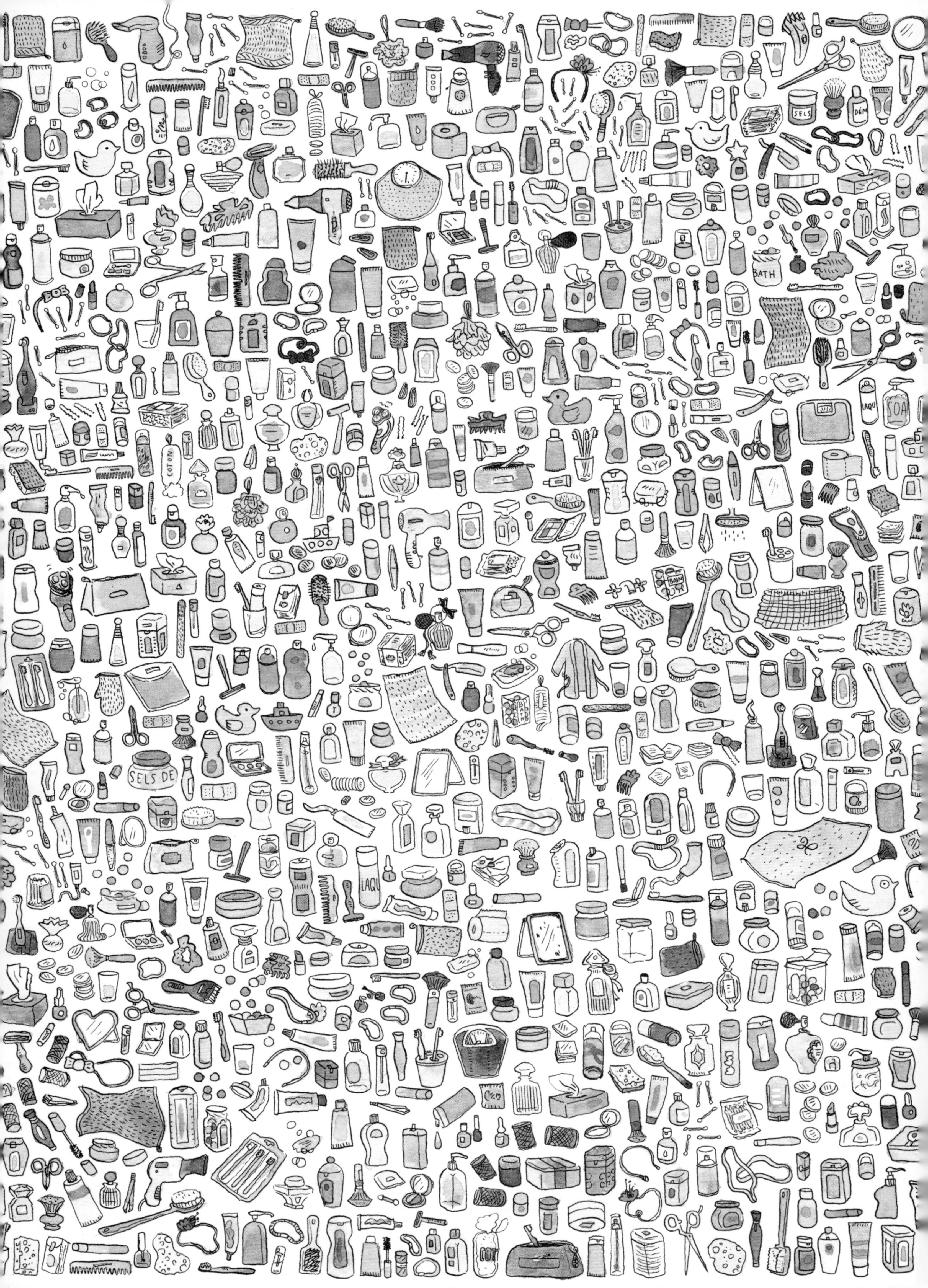
SELS
DÉM
BATH
LAQU
SOA
COTON
BAIN
GEL
SELS DE
LAQU

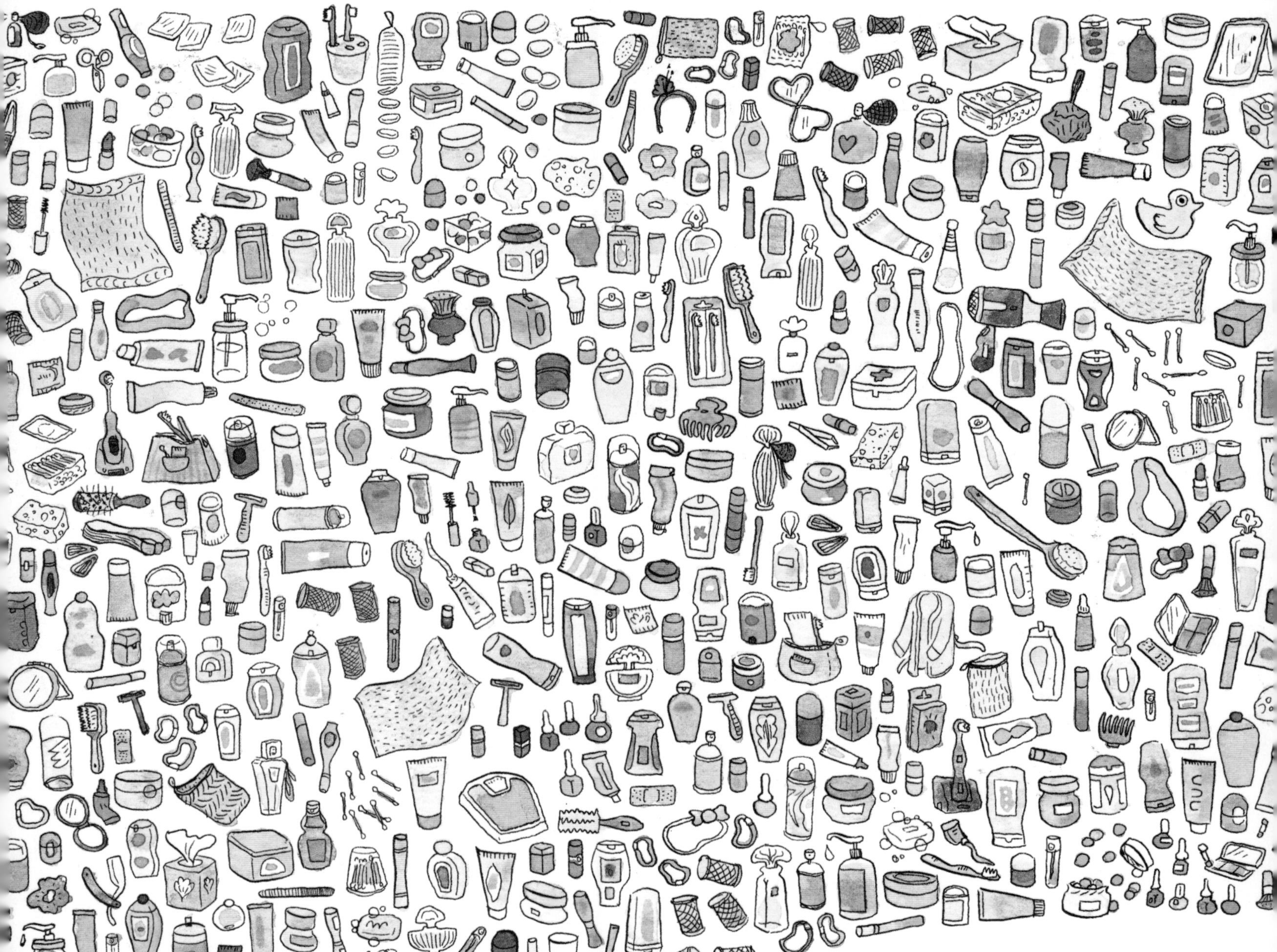

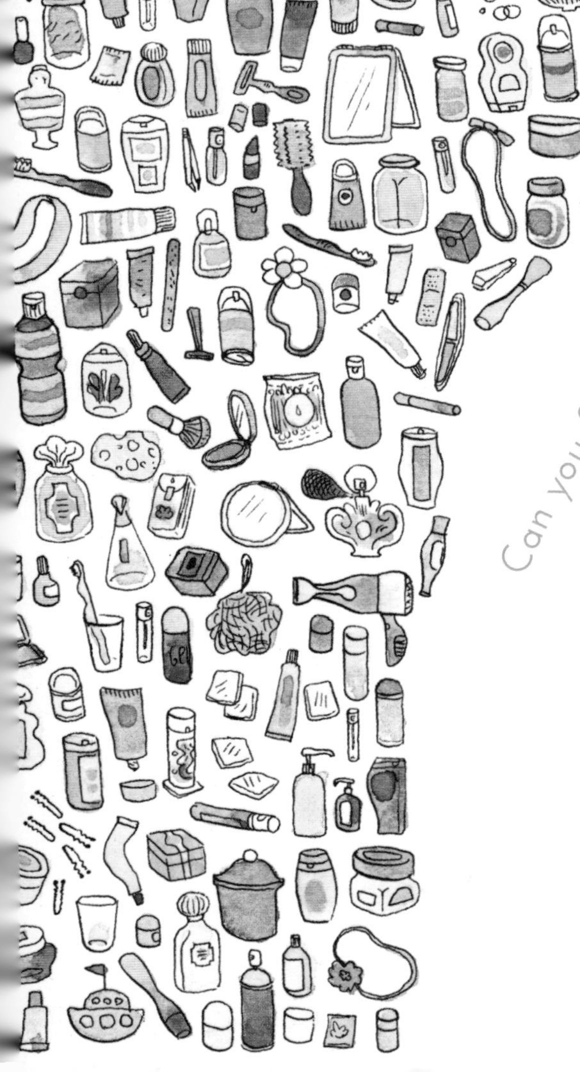

Can you find the 6 rubber ducks I play with?

Then in the bathroom, I can choose between spreading a thick layer of shampoo on my hair or making a fake beard out of shaving foam.

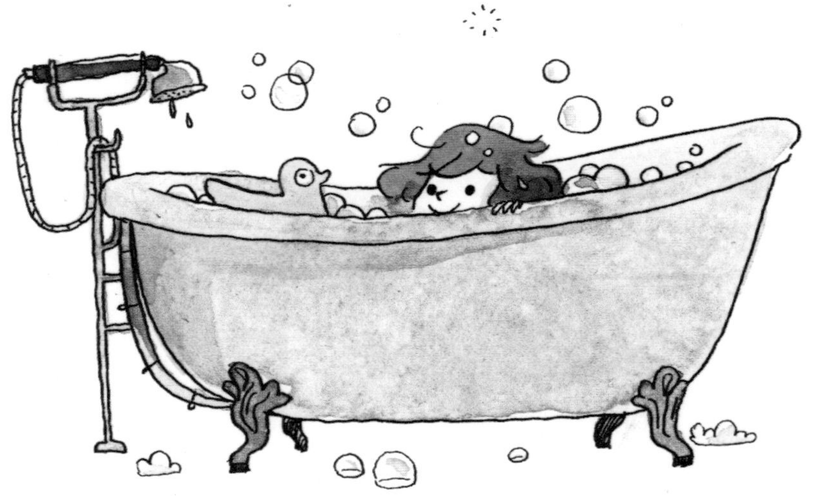

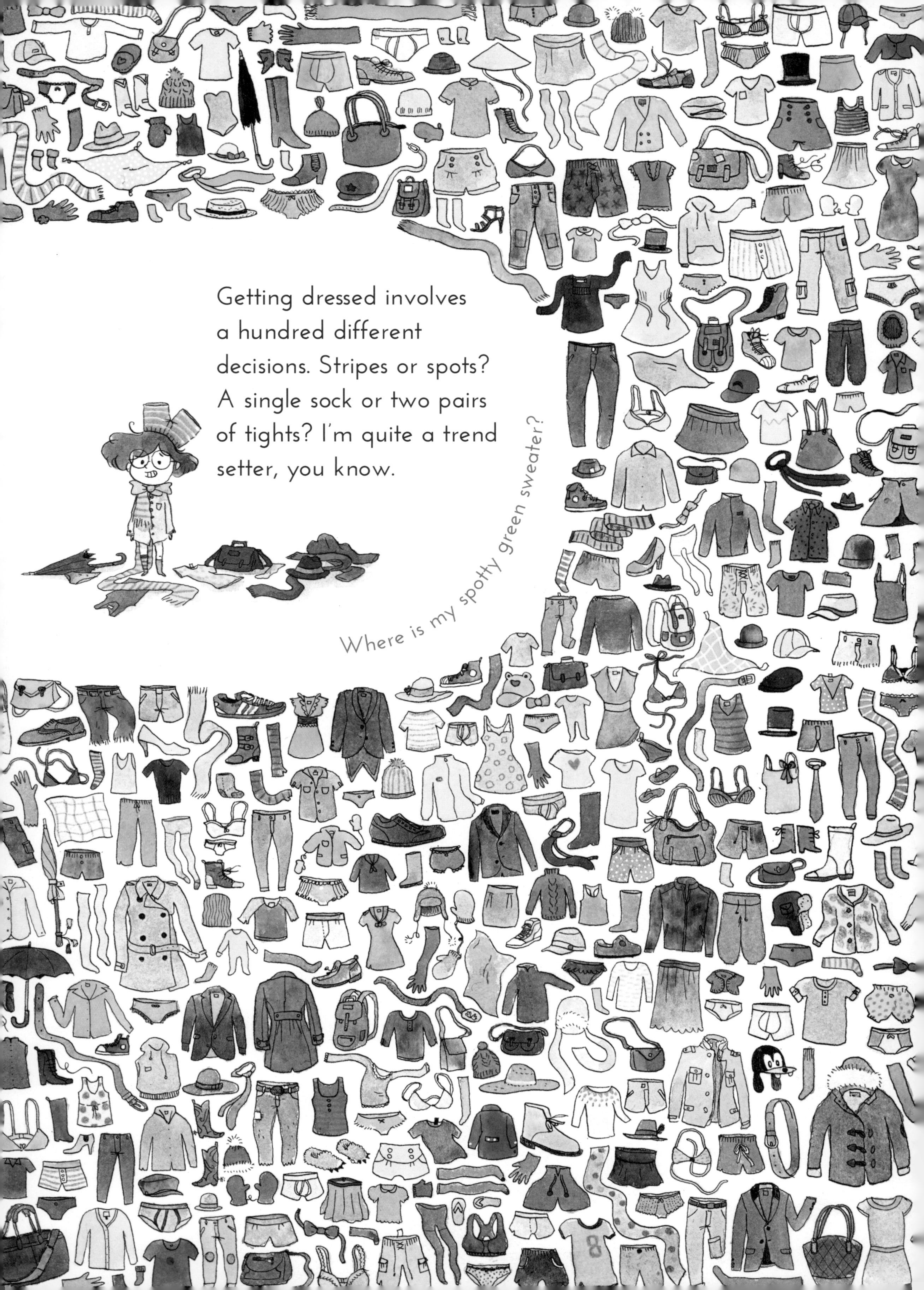
Getting dressed involves a hundred different decisions. Stripes or spots? A single sock or two pairs of tights? I'm quite a trend setter, you know.
Where is my spotty green sweater?

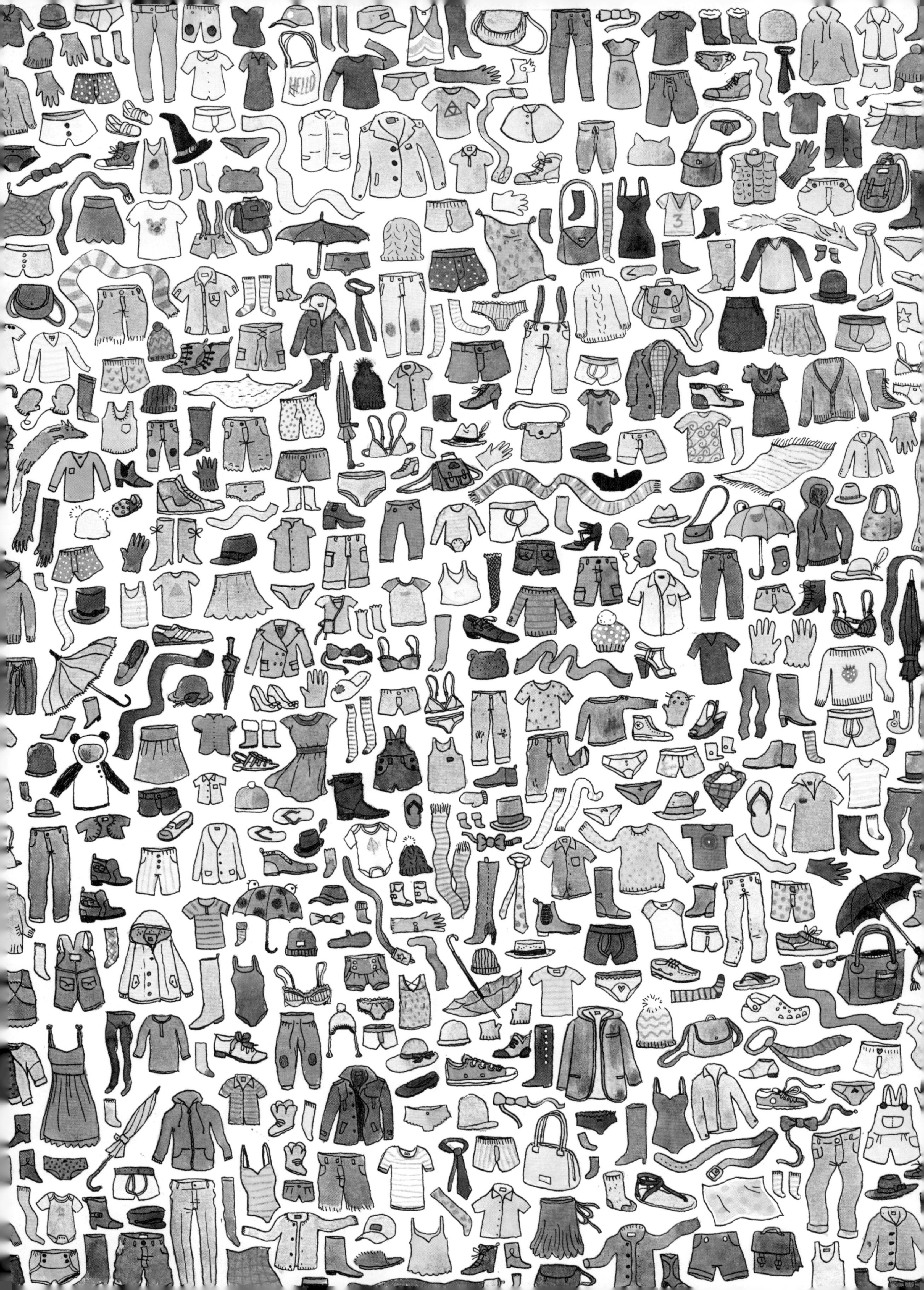
HELLO

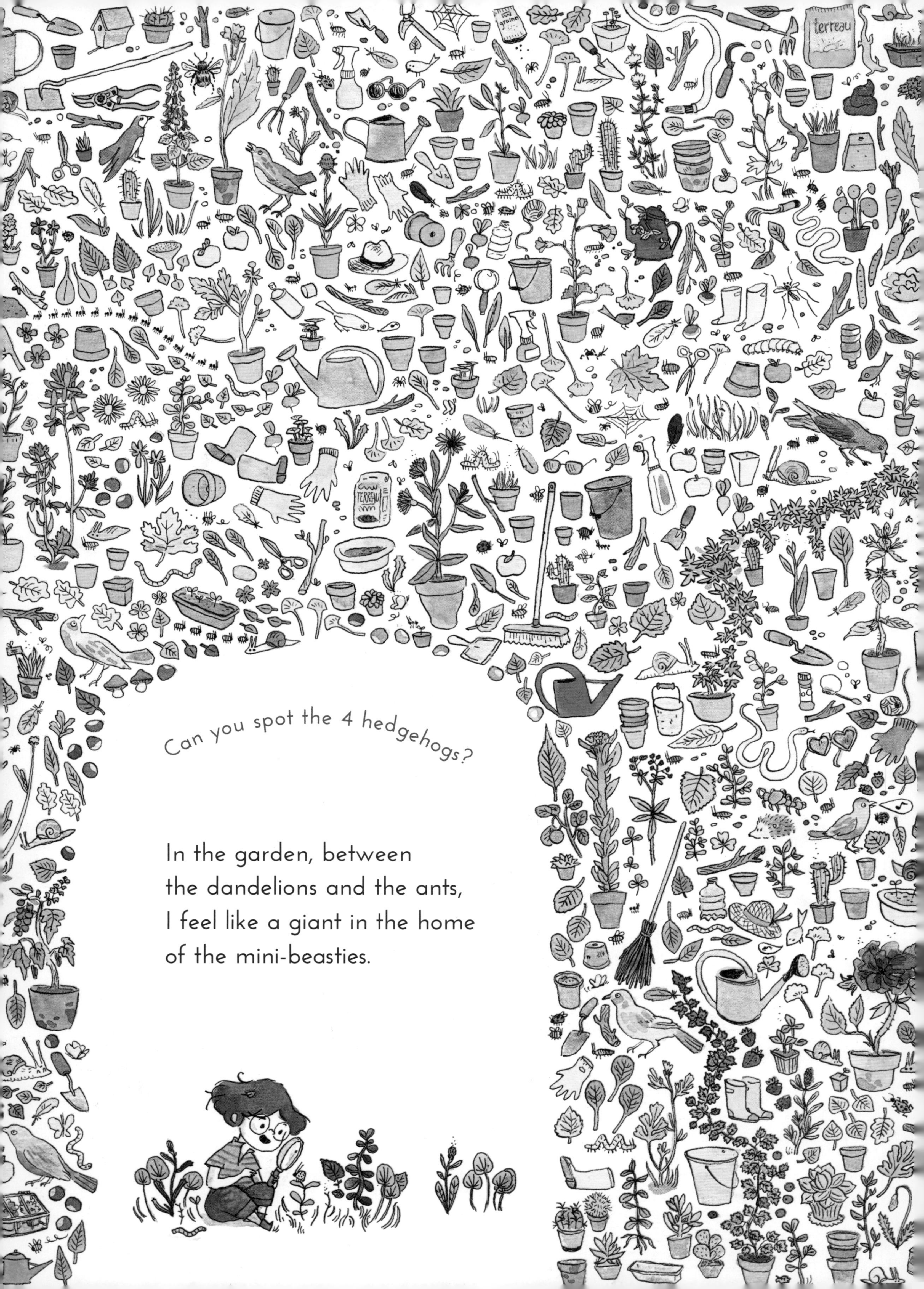

Can you spot the 4 hedgehogs?

In the garden, between
the dandelions and the ants,
I feel like a giant in the home
of the mini-beasties.

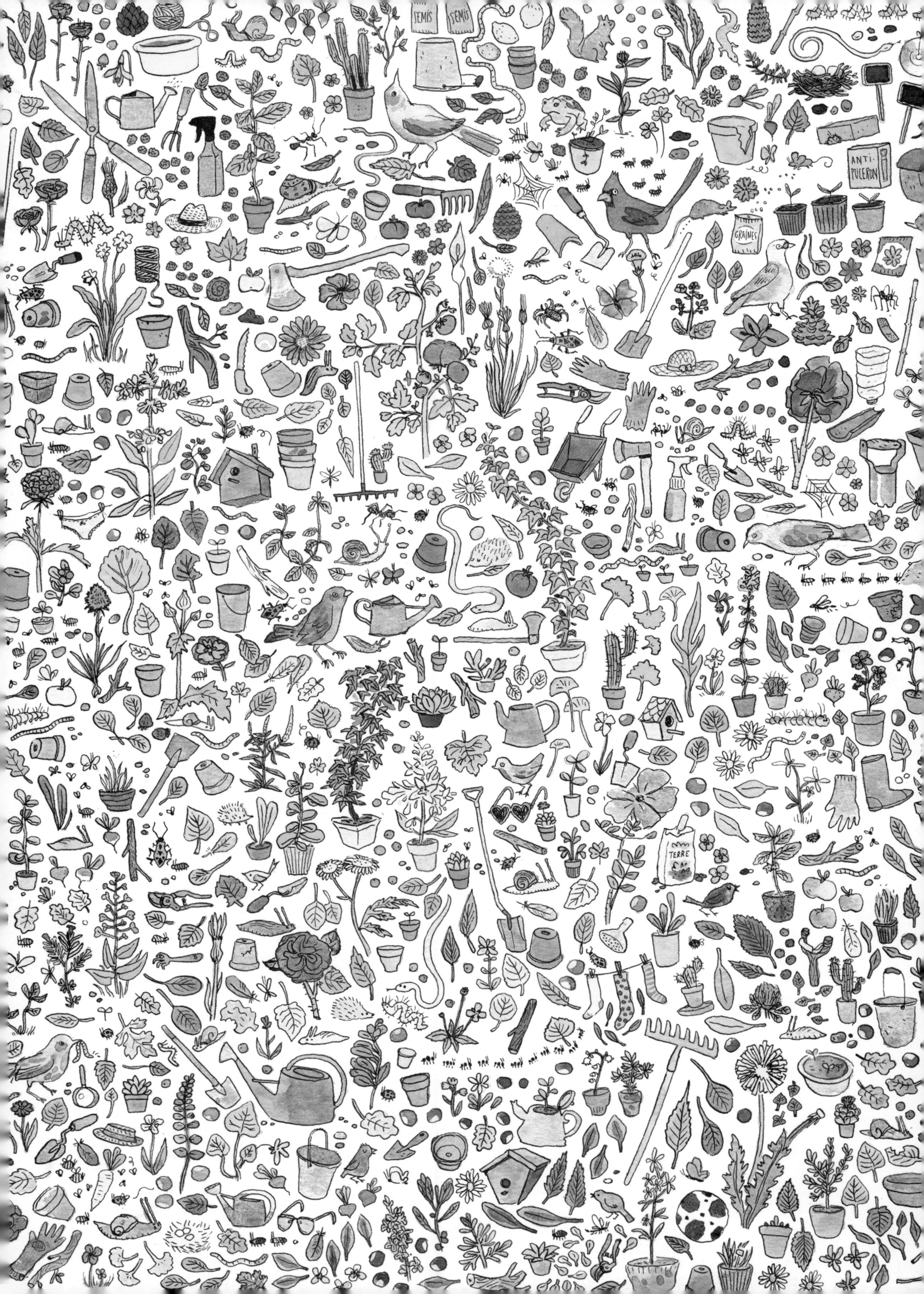
SEMIS
SEMIS
ANTI-PUCERON
GRAINES
TERRE

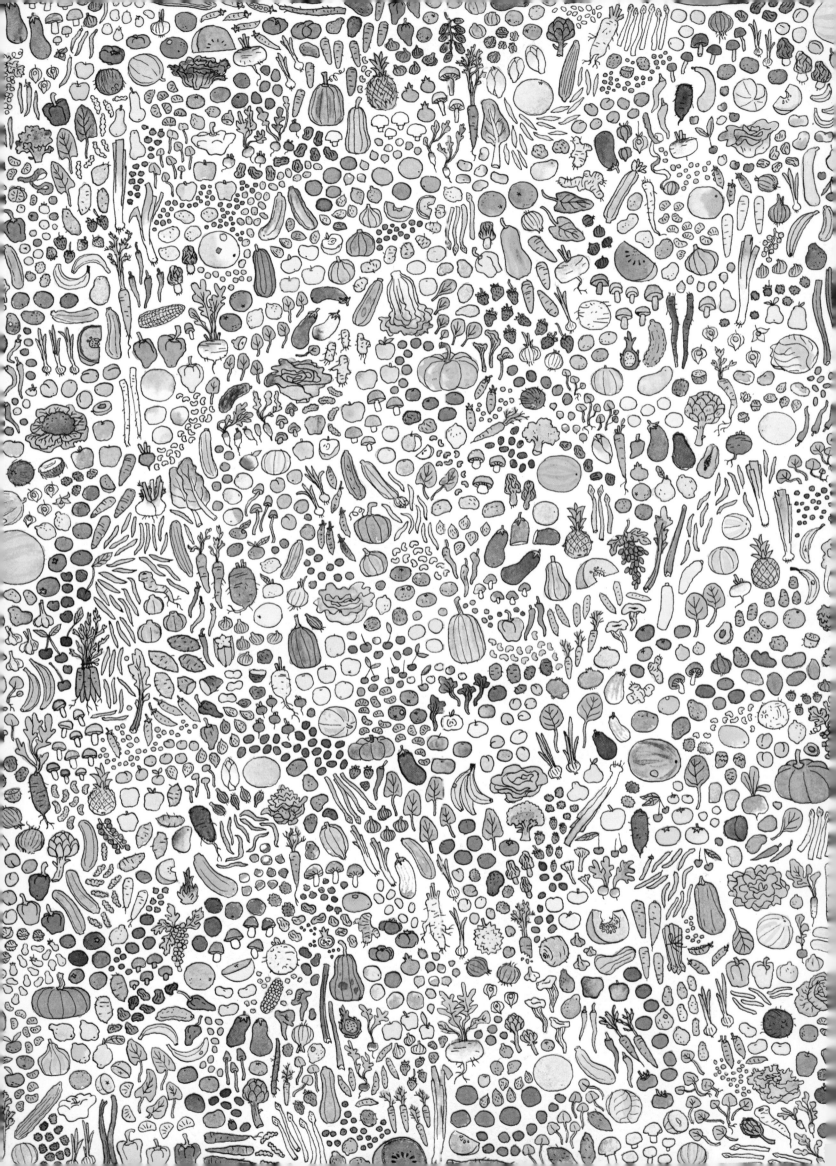

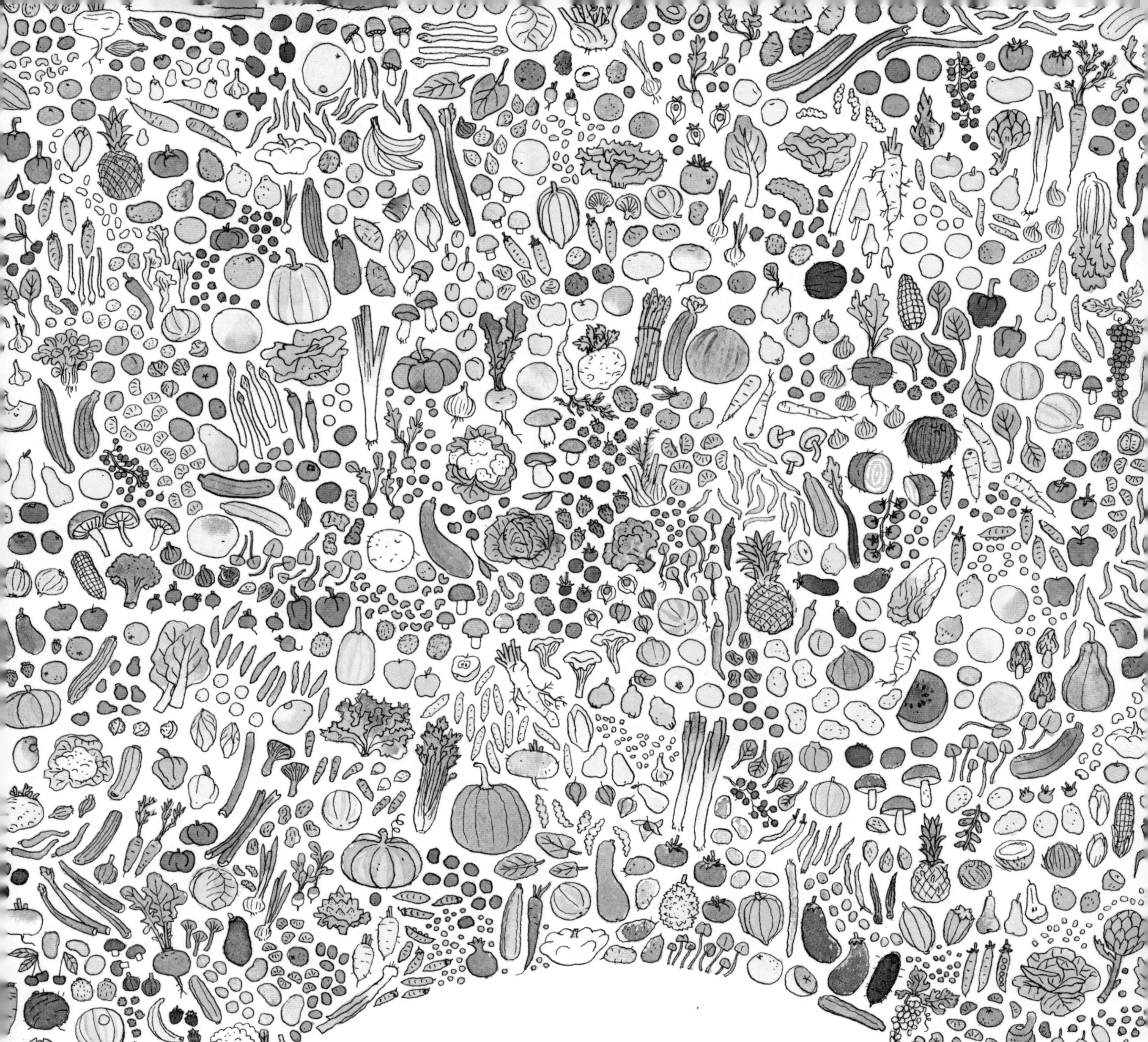

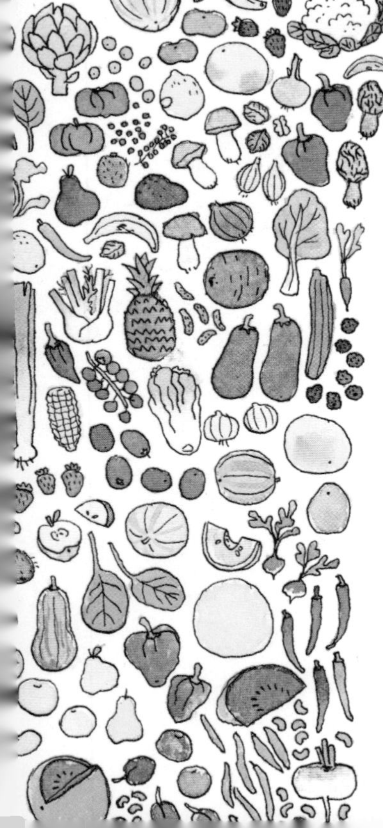

Every Saturday, Mom and I go to the market. It's a heavenly place where I can taste a bit of everything, for free! (If I ask nicely ...).

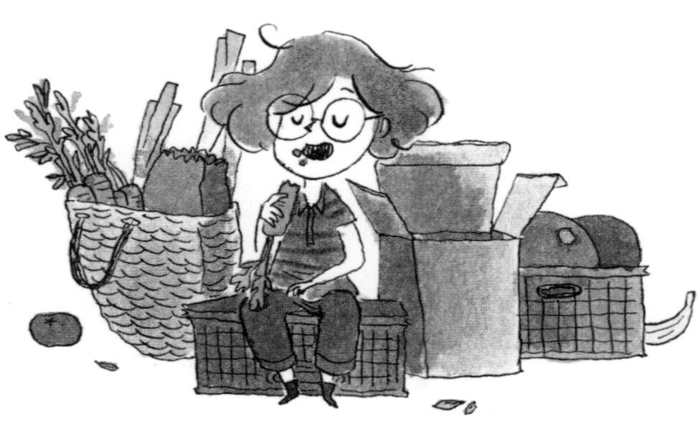

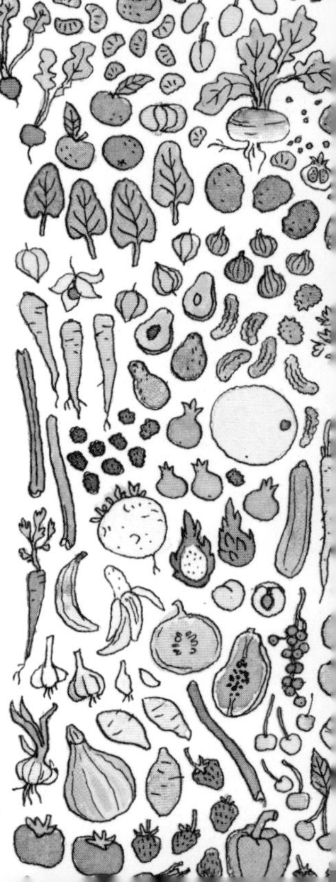

Find the nibbled carrot!

Then, we go to MY store, where things go *KABOOM!* and *RING RING!* when you press their thingamajig. I love it!

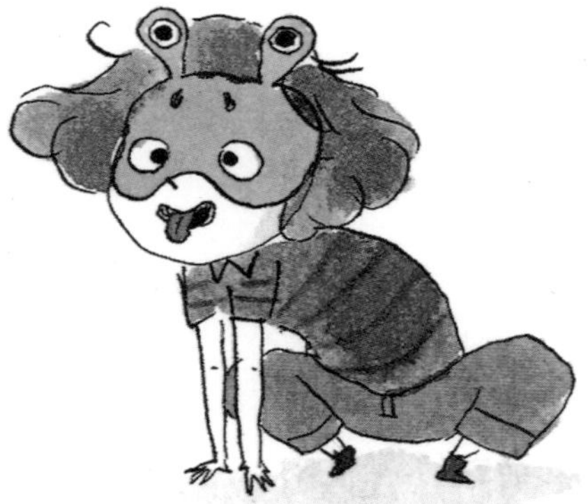

Can you find the frog mask I'm wearing?

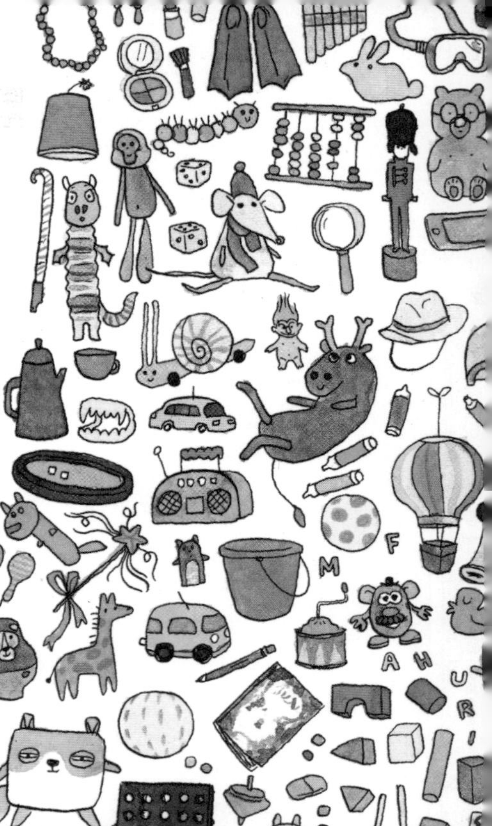

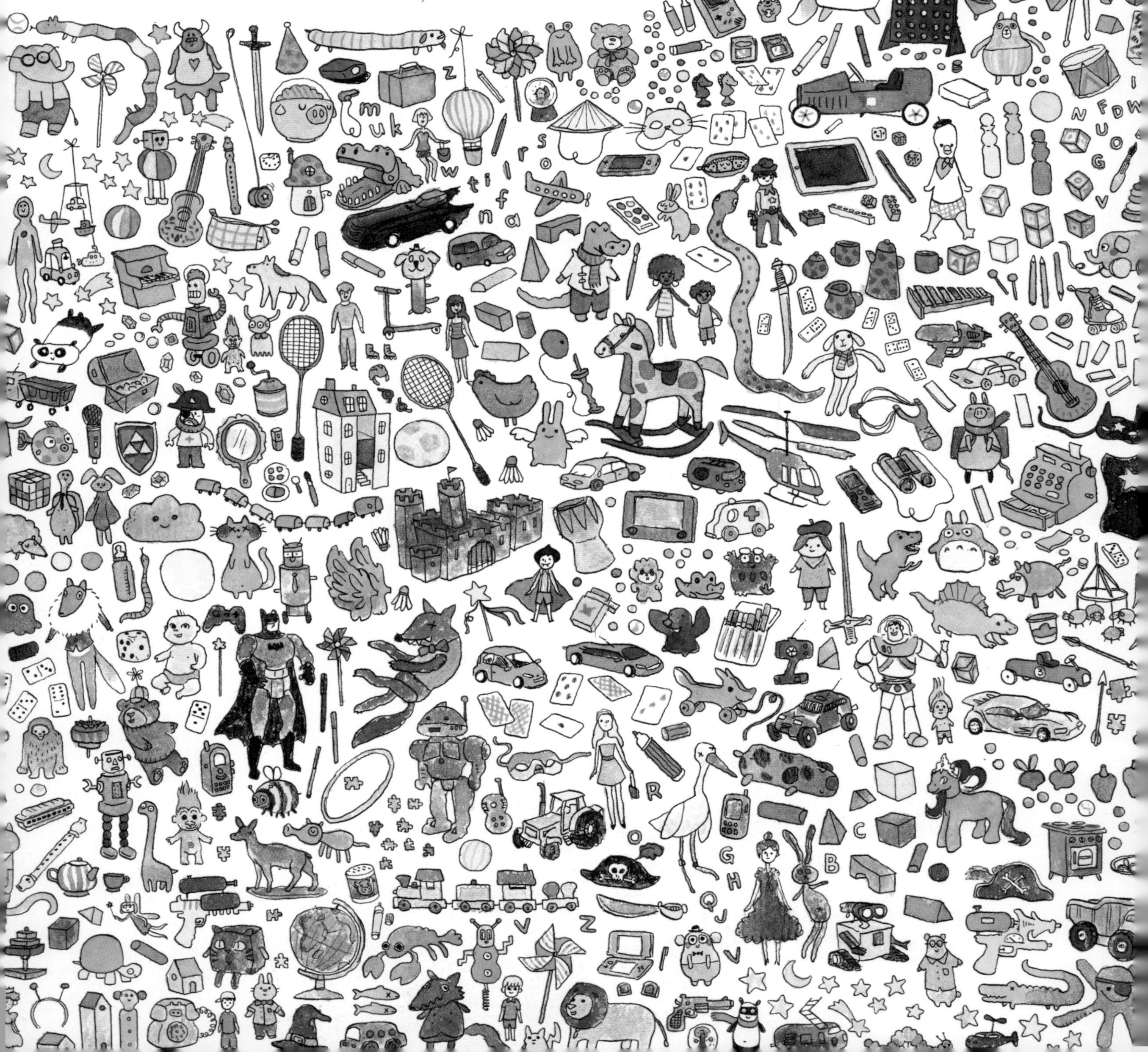

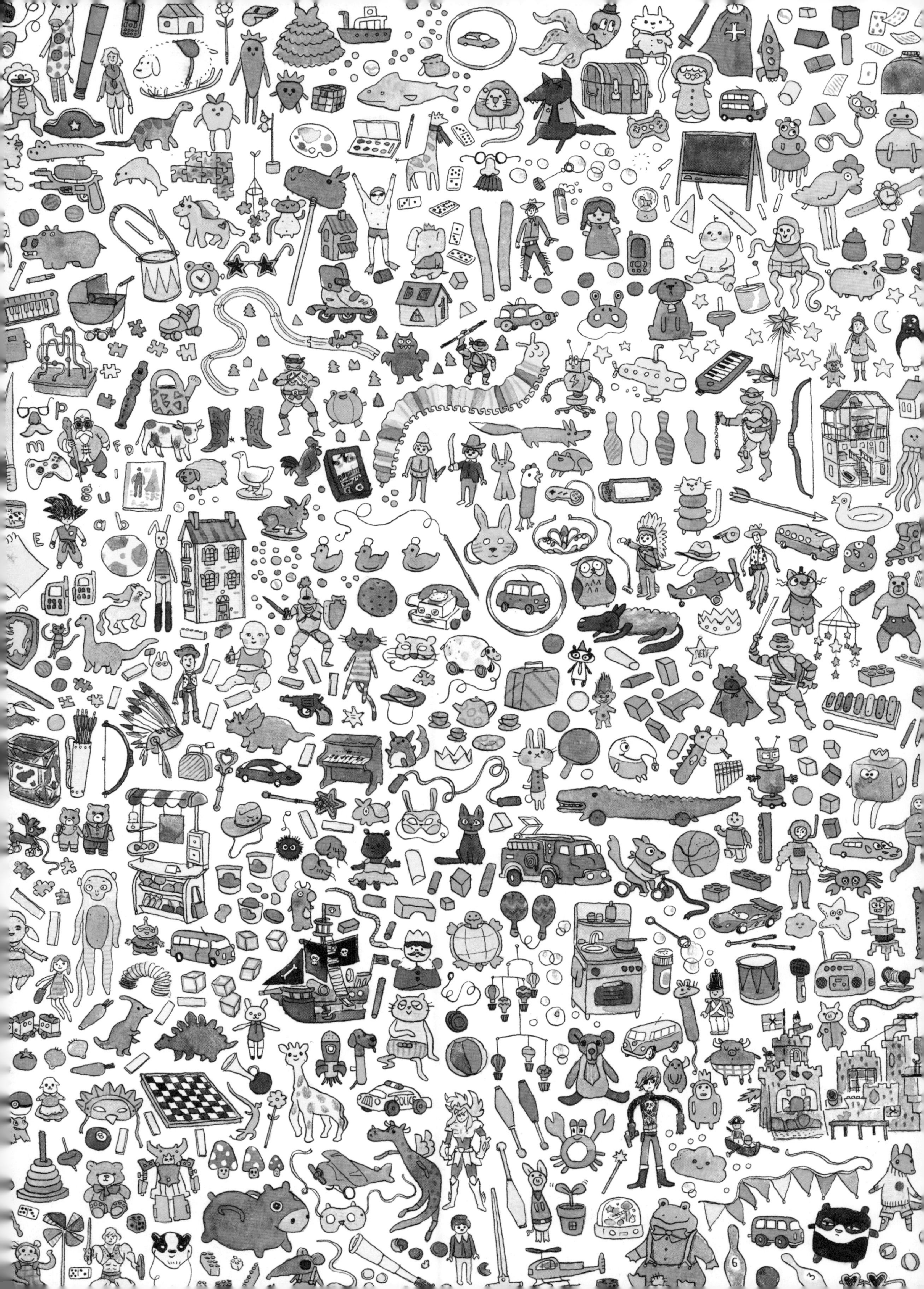
POLICE

When it's snack time,
in front of the bakery,
I wonder if all this choice
is an eternal delight
or an infernal torment.
So *BANG!* I just
take a gamble!

Yum, a pyramid of cream cakes! Can you see it?

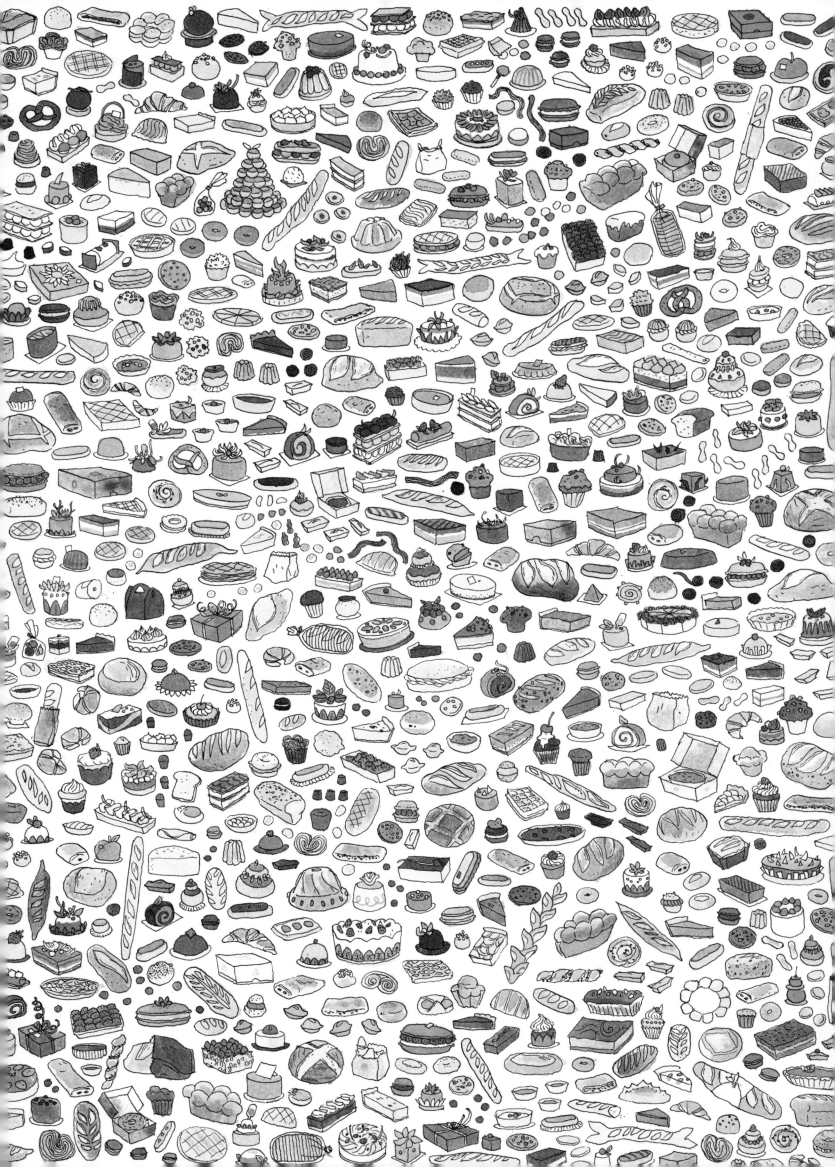

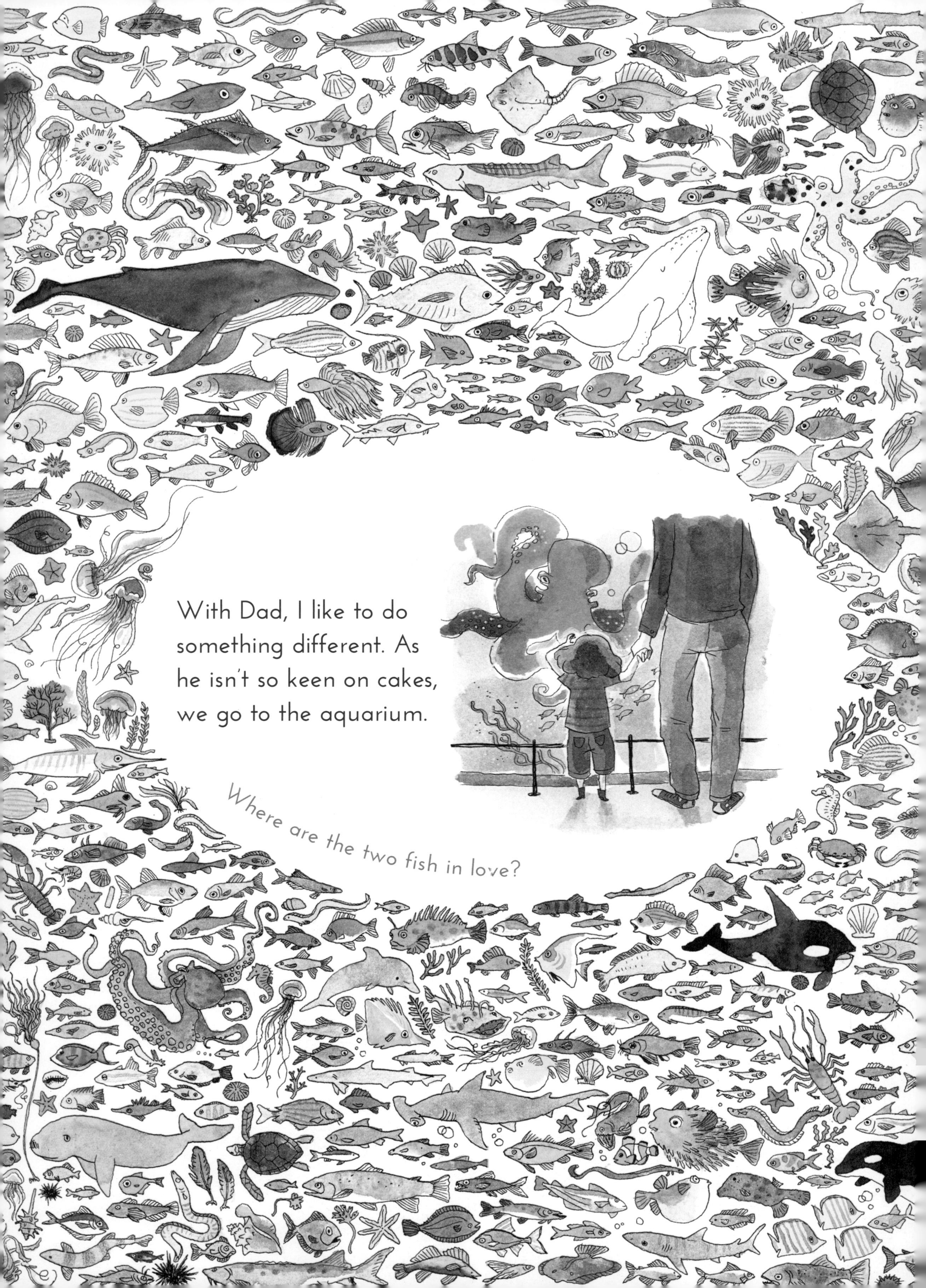

With Dad, I like to do something different. As he isn't so keen on cakes, we go to the aquarium.

Where are the two fish in love?

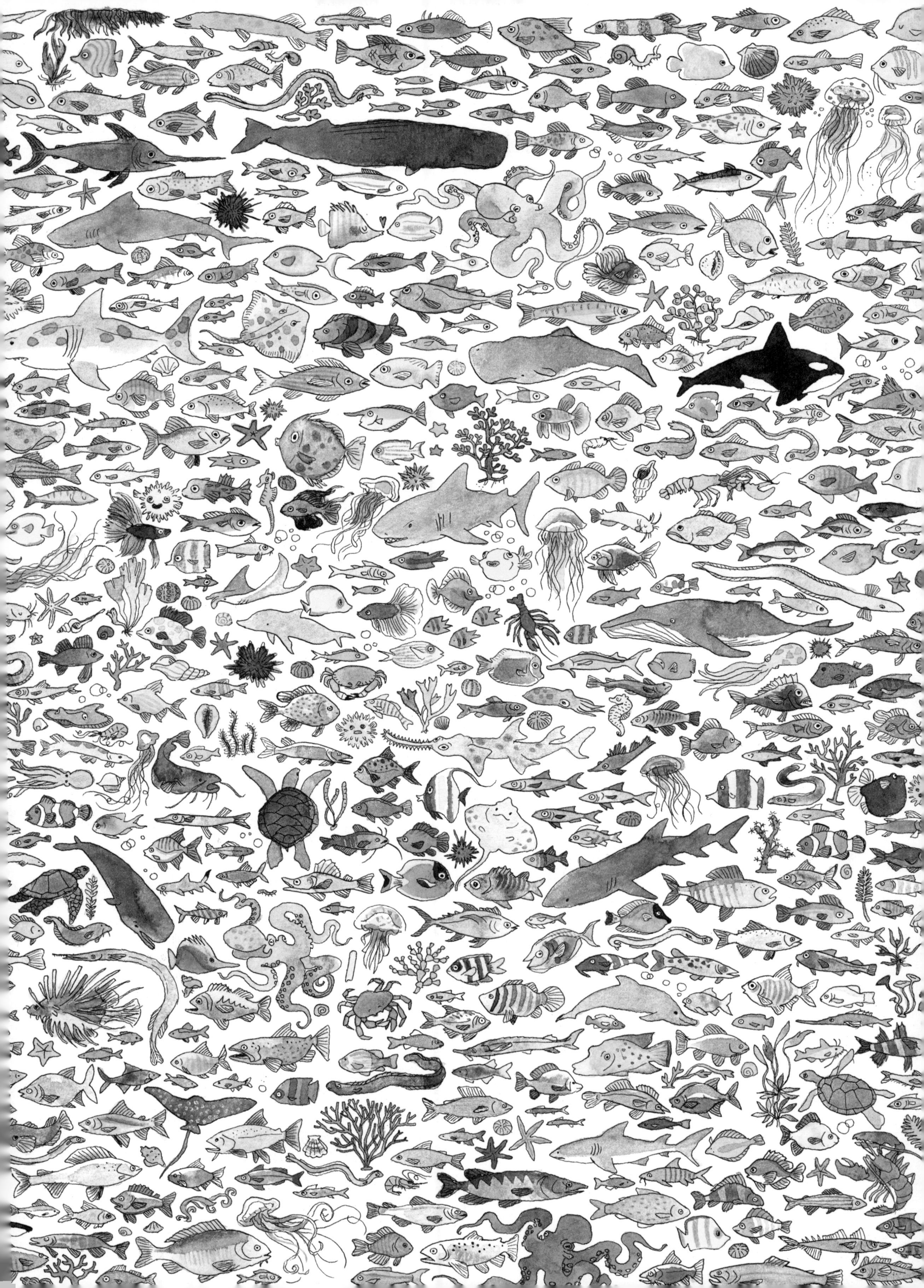

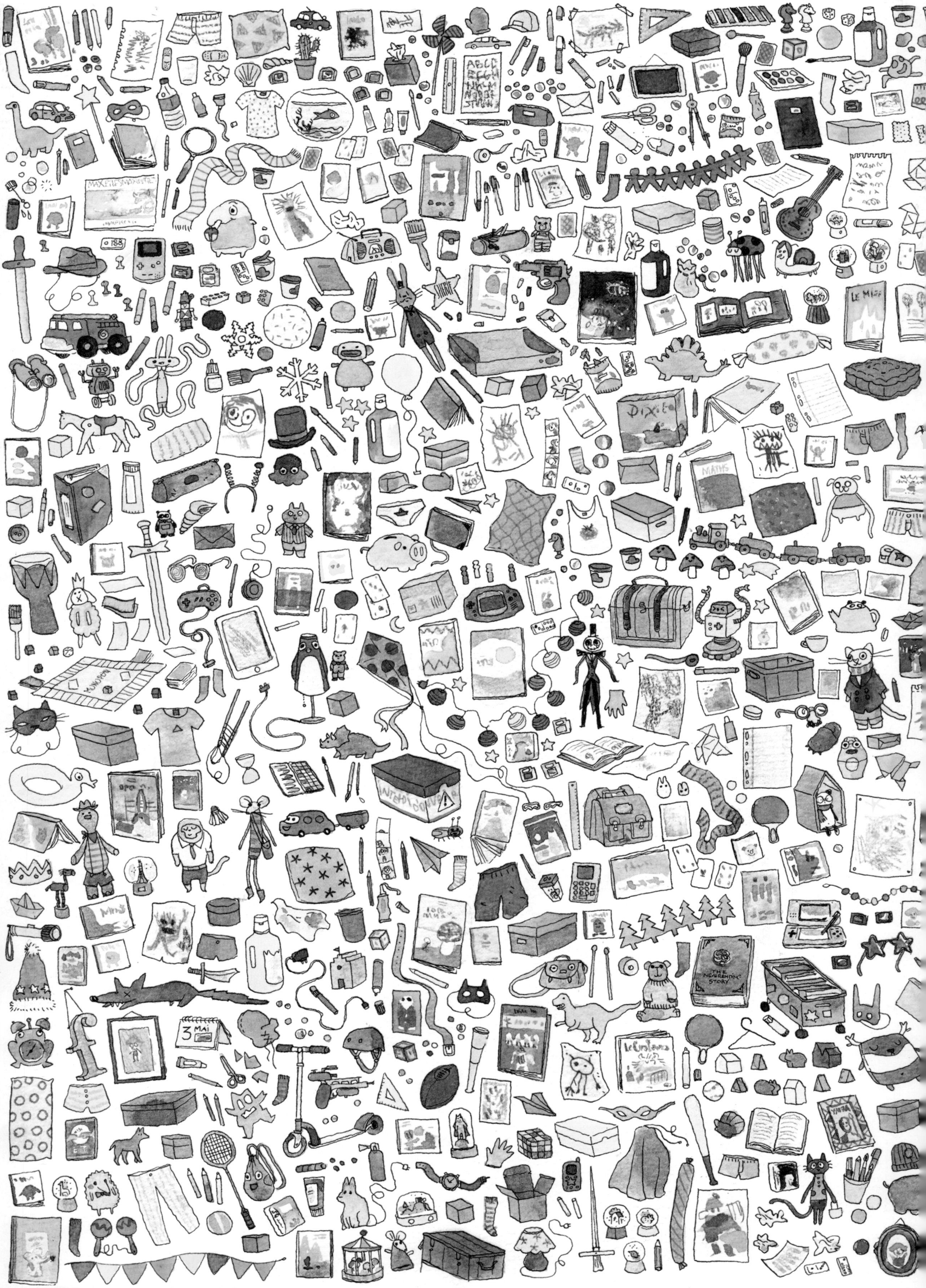
MATHS
3 MAI
THE NEVERENDING STORY

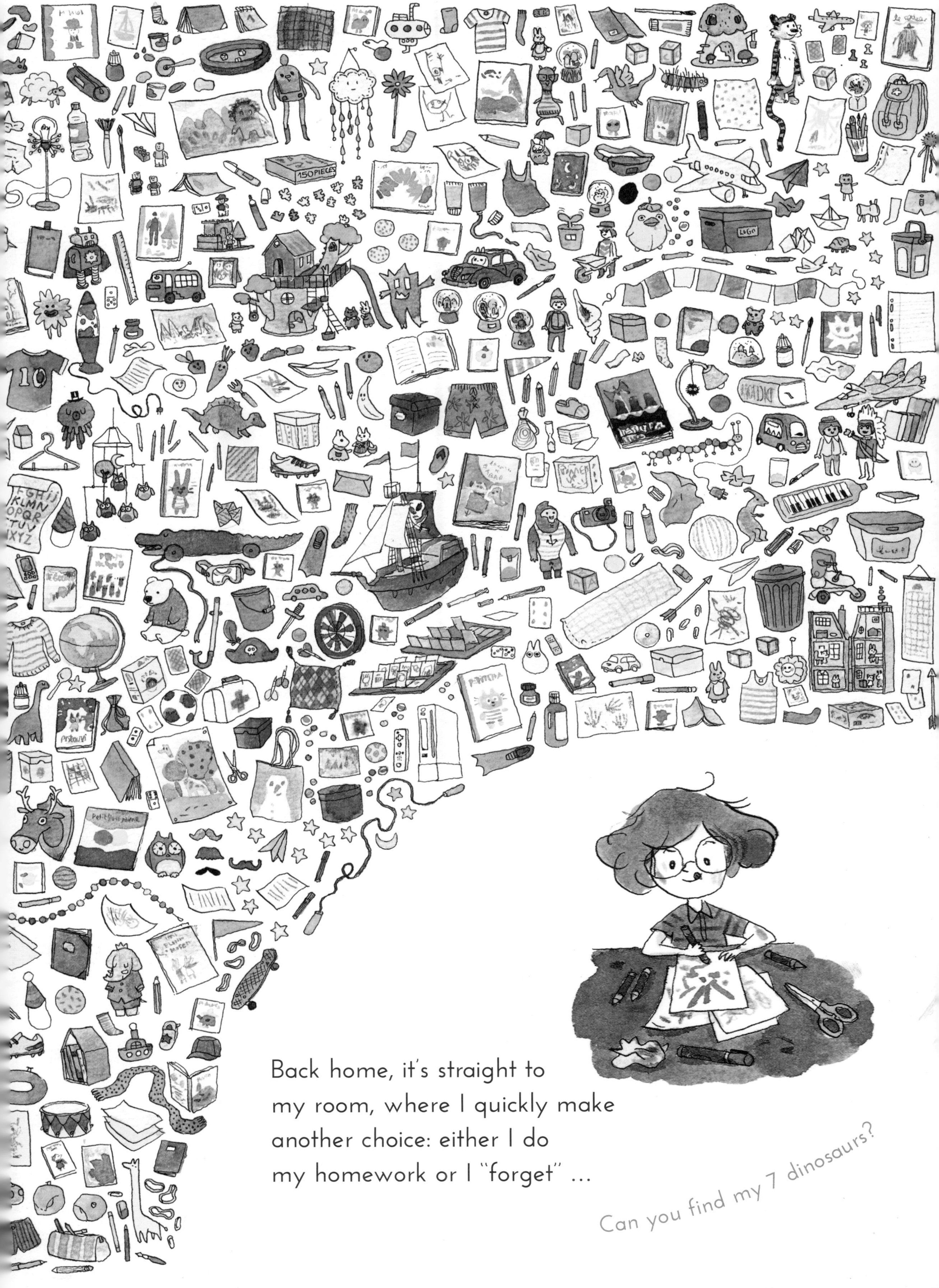

Back home, it's straight to
my room, where I quickly make
another choice: either I do
my homework or I "forget" ...

Can you find my 7 dinosaurs?

At dinner time, Dad always prepares delicious dishes, but he can be a bit absent-minded. Too sweet? Too salty? Too spicy? Too burnt? You never know what you're going to get!

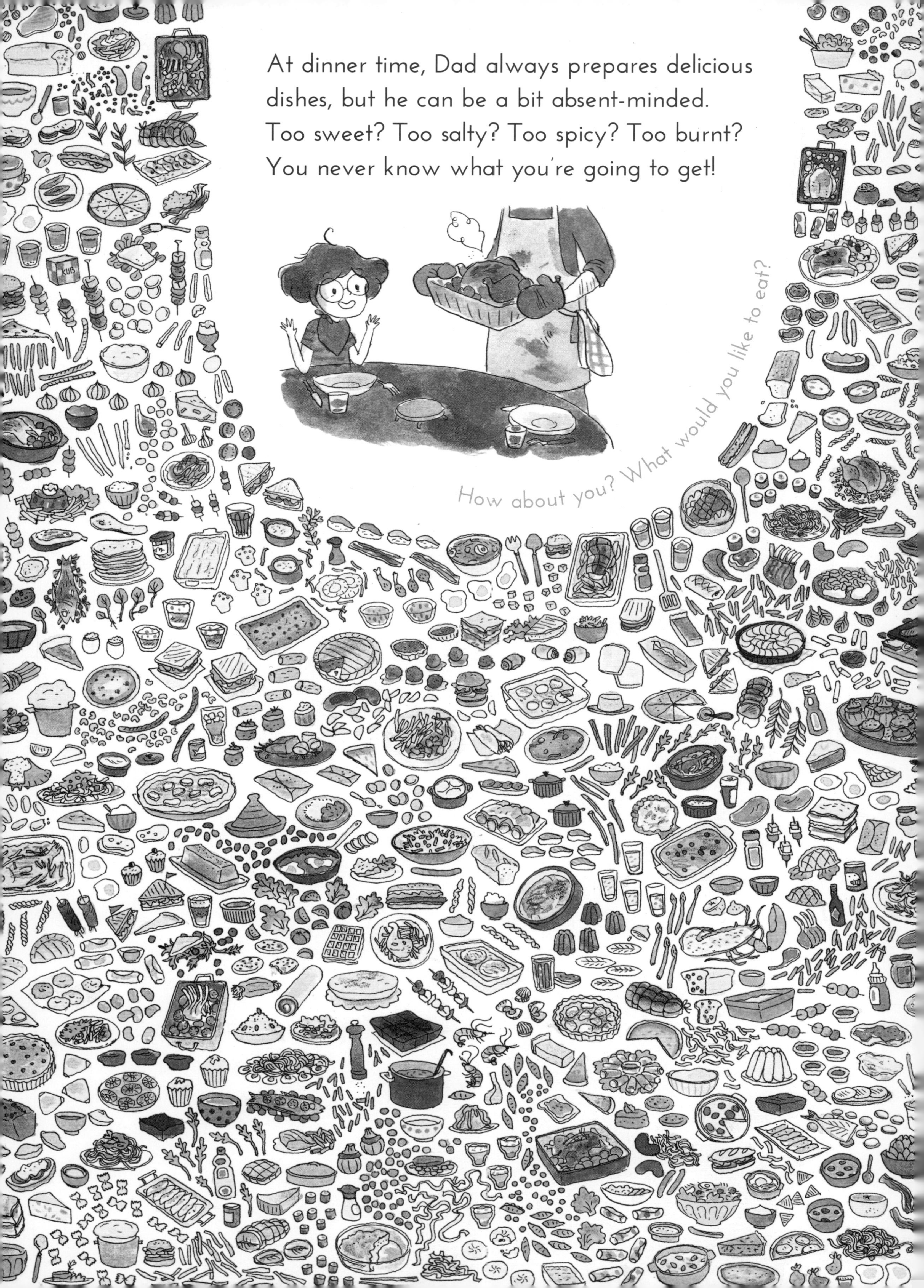

How about you? What would you like to eat?

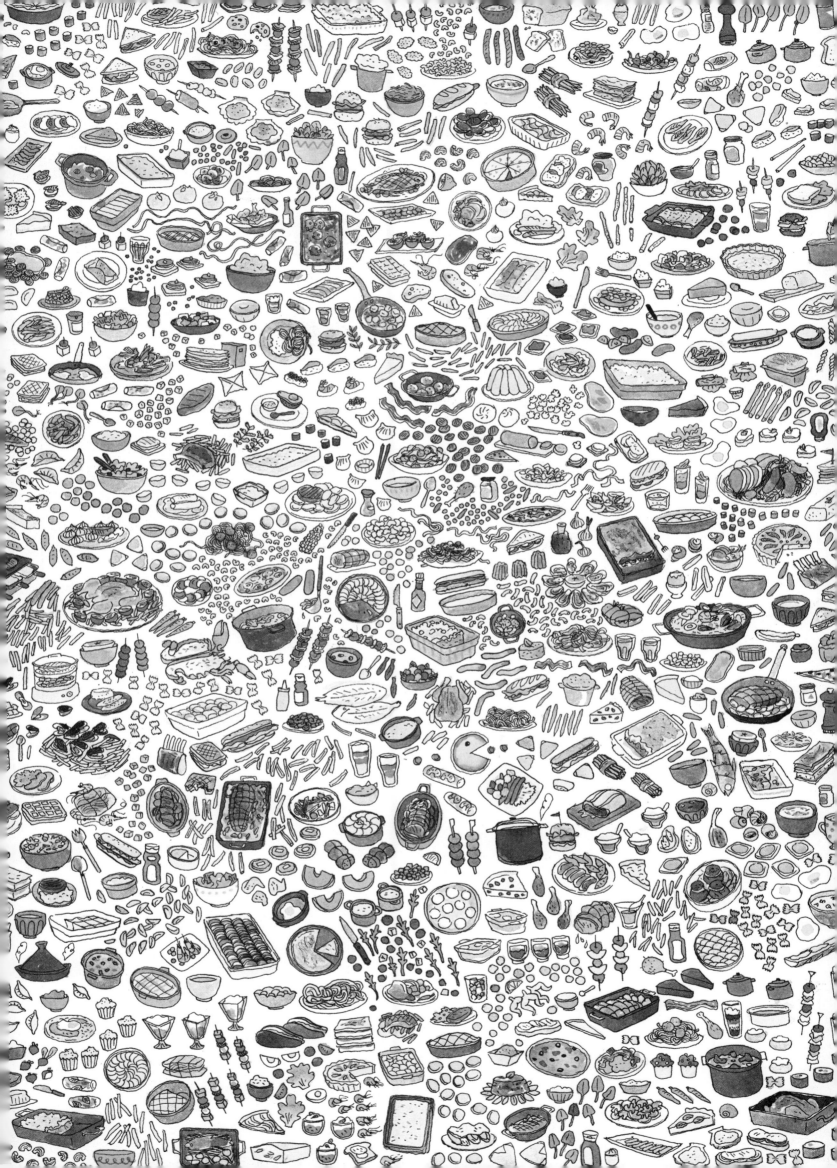

So, you see, after all those different things to do and choose between during the day, once I get into bed it's a complete nightmare!

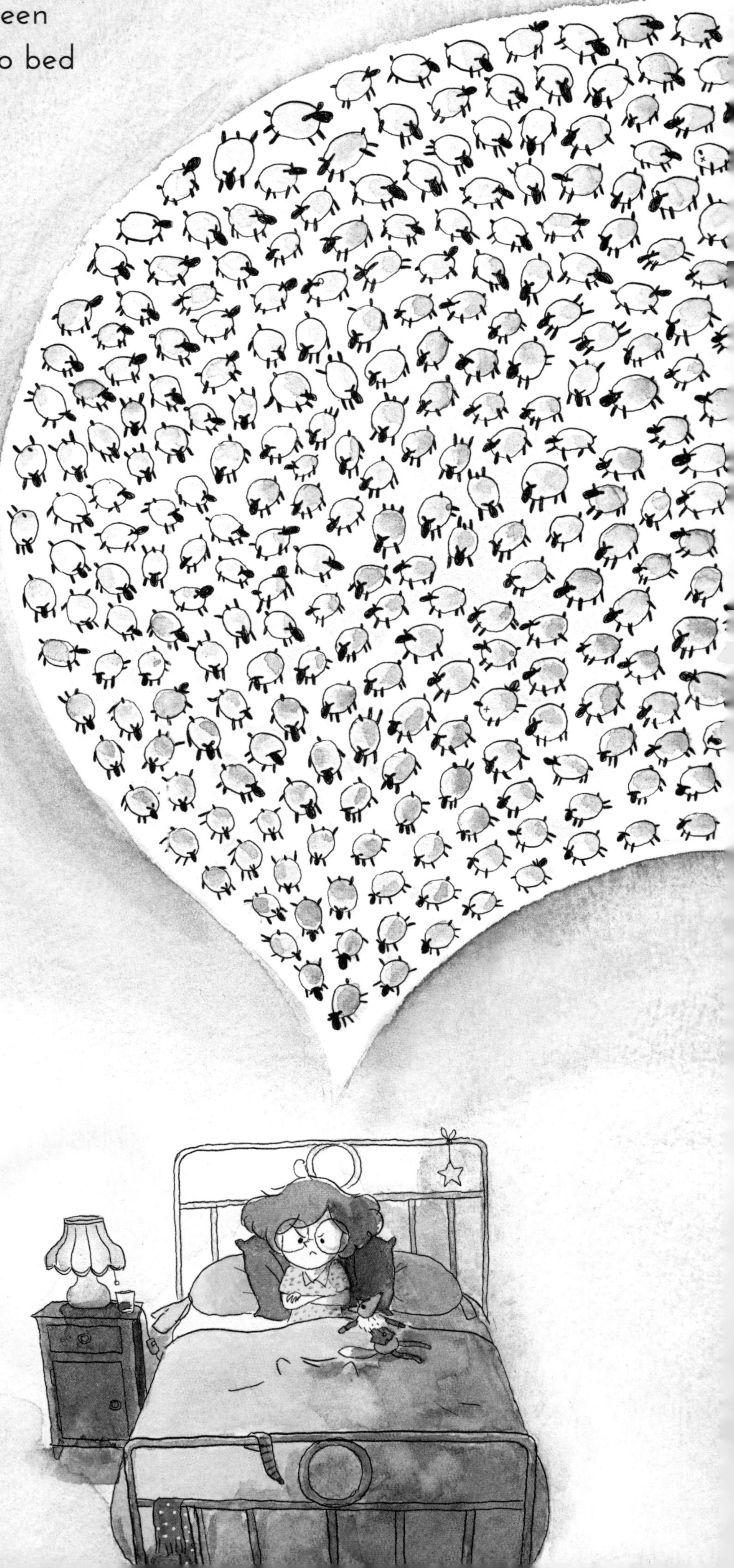

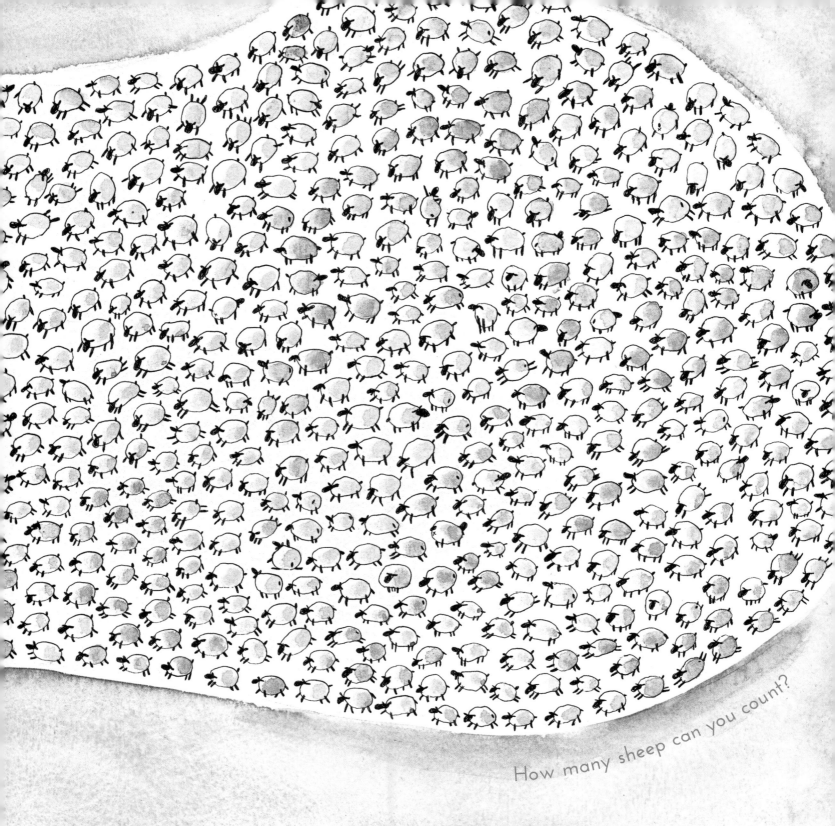

How many sheep can you count?

Sheep.

Nothing but sheep ...

Always the same old boring sheep!

WHERE'S THE FUN IN THAT?

Solutions

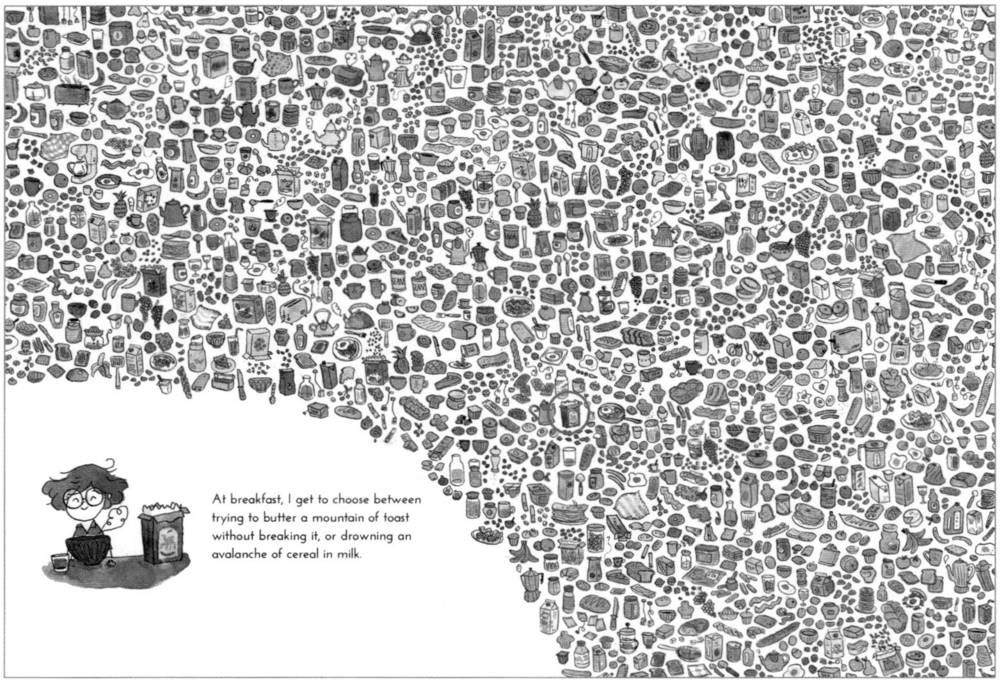
At breakfast, I get to choose between trying to butter a mountain of toast without breaking it, or drowning an avalanche of cereal in milk.

Can you find my box of breakfast cereal?

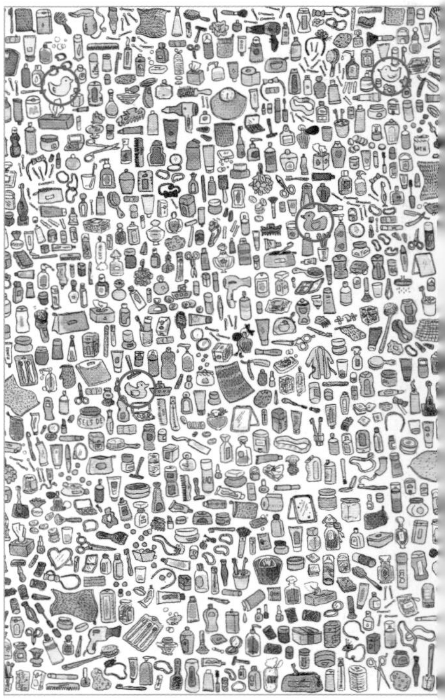

Can you find the 6 rubbe

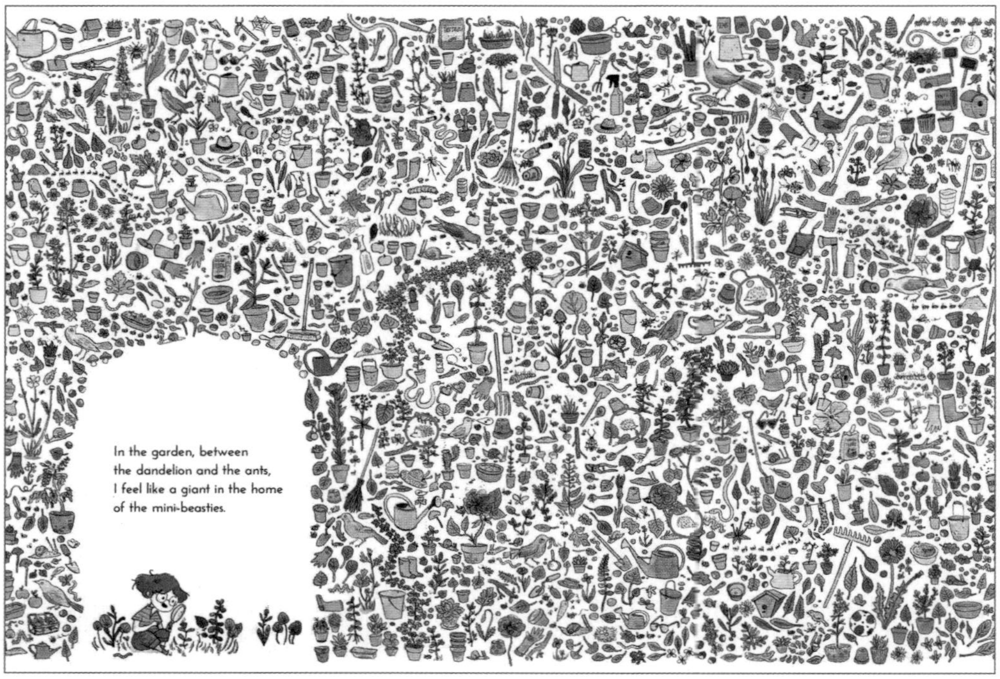
In the garden, between the dandelion and the ants, I feel like a giant in the home of the mini-beasties.

Can you spot the 4 hedgehogs?

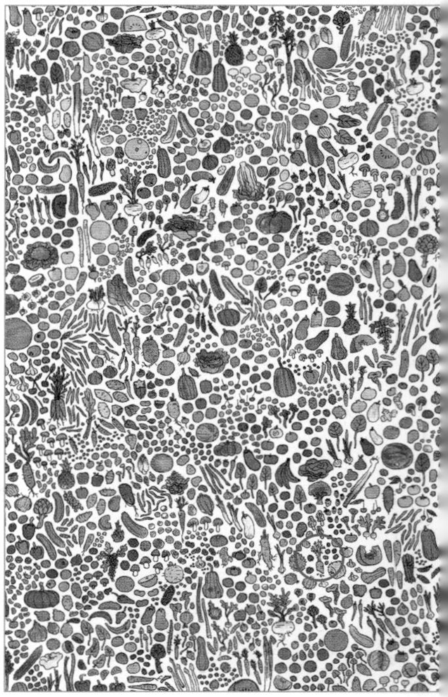

Find the nibbled carrot!

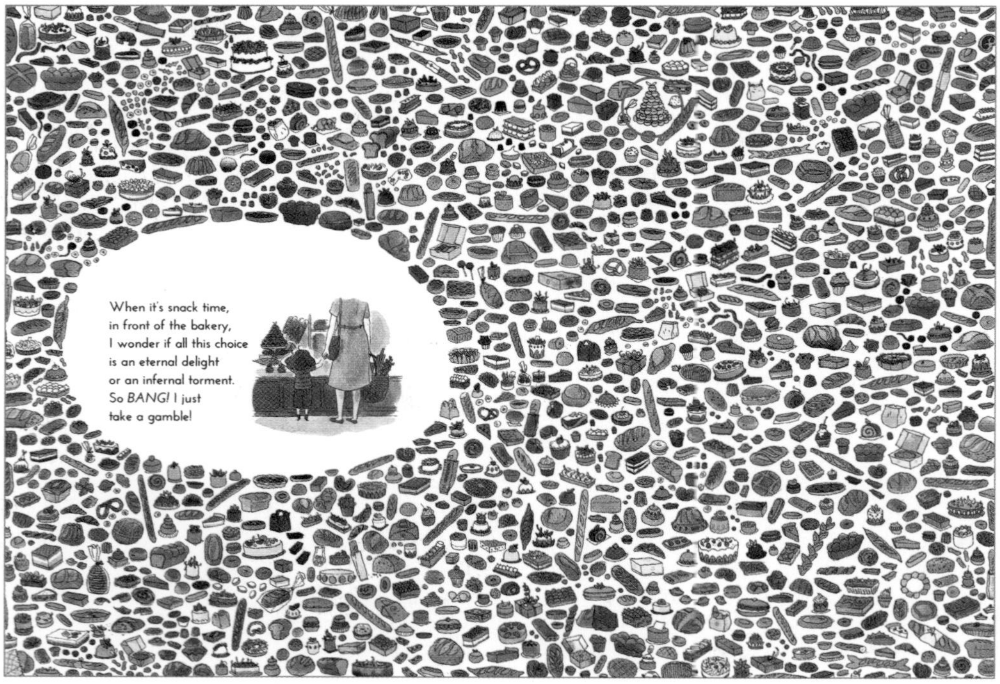
When it's snack time, in front of the bakery, I wonder if all this choice is an eternal delight or an infernal torment. So *BANG!* I just take a gamble!

Yum, a pyramid of cream cakes! Can you see it?

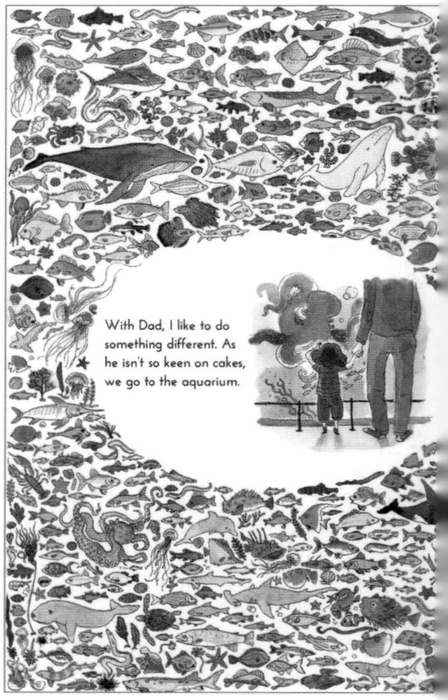
With Dad, I like to do something different. As he isn't so keen on cakes, we go to the aquarium.

Where are the two fish i